THROUGH THE WINDOW PANE

Stories in 100 Words

BY JAMES M. DUPREE

Illustrations by
KATHLEEN DUPREE

Acknowledgments

I want to thank my wonderful partner, Abigail, for her love, support, and exceptional talent for titling things (including this book and some of its stories). Thank you to my mother, Kathleen, for providing the beautiful illustrations within this book. And thank you to everyone who has supported my writing endeavors, whether it be through kind words, constructive criticism, likes on Instagram, or the purchase of this book.

Table of Contents

· 1 ·

Through the Window Pane

There is a window, a relic passed down from family I barely knew. I keep it for one reason alone. When the sun has reached its peak, the light hits the glass pane, performing a prismatic dance before shifting into solid forms. I see living things and places from this world and others. I hear voices travel through this crystalline portal. I witness their stories through their eyes.

When days are long, and I need a brief moment of respite, I look through the glass. Expectation is a fool's game, as I never know what the window will show me.

· 2 ·

A Cold Night

Eight hours on the road, and Darryl was feeling hungry. Fortunately, Mel's diner was open 24 hours, but it seemed everyone had got up and left. Hot meals were left to cool while eggs burned in the pan. Purses, coats, and vehicles were abandoned. Maybe this was the Rapture, Darryl thought. Why wasn't he taken? He called out, but silence was the only reply.

Darryl grabbed the silver cross hung around his neck and ran back to his rig. And for the people who had been robbed and locked in the freezer, they had a cold night ahead of them.

GRAND RE-OPENING

· 3 ·

The Regal Hill

In 1988, the Regal Hill Mall was constructed near the town center of Bartlet, NC. Locals flocked to the shopping center for years, proving the mall to be a success. But then times changed, and malls slowly died out. Ownership switched hands, and reopenings floundered.

In 2025, as Regal Hill began foreclosure proceedings, the world went to war with itself. In the ashes, the mall miraculously stood strong. One of the last few buildings intact, survivors naturally found solace under its roof. A community formed and grew. Tradesmen talked, and word traveled. The people flocked to Regal Hill once more.

WANTED
FOR VANDALISM

· 4 ·

The Defense

Mr. Barley was noticeably sweating. Once again, his clients had not arrived at their trial, and the judge was growing irate. The court had posted summons signs all around town and even read them aloud in the fields. There would be no more delays. "This is their last chance at defense before being punished for their repeated crimes of crop vandalism," said the judge.

Mr. Barley silently prayed for a miracle. Then screams echoed from outside as a black furry mass of rats scurried through the town and into the courthouse. "It seems my clients have arrived!" said Mr. Barley.

· 5 ·

With Great Power

Jack sat dismayed at his new cellmate, whose tongue voraciously fondled the bars of their cell. "The hell ya doing?" asked Jack.

"I got powers," said his cellmate, taking brief pauses. "Saliva is corrosive. Outta here in no time."

"Always gettin' the freaks," mumbled Jack.

A week passed. Jack noticed the bars appeared slimmer but was convinced it was an illusion. A simple trick of the light. Late into the night, he heard the ring of broken metal and leapt from his bed. He was alone, the cell bars lying on the floor. Jack learned to appreciate his weirder cellmates.

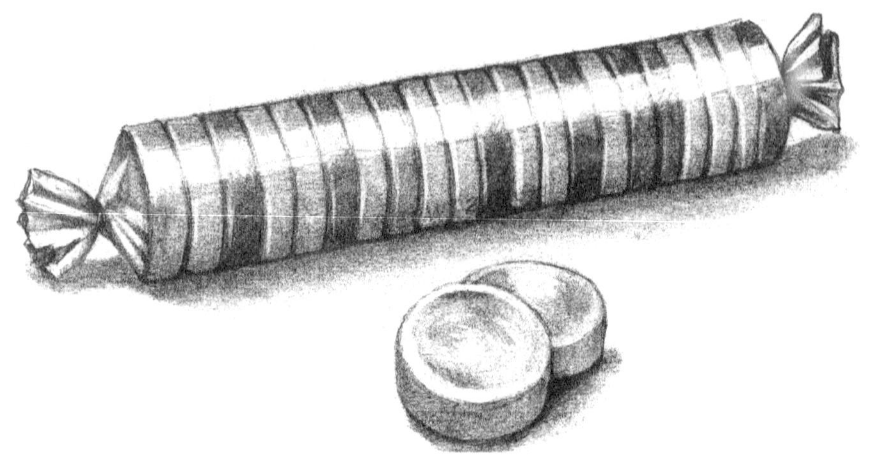

· 6 ·

One at a Time

Tishanna sat on the front steps of her Meemaw's porch and threw a handful of Smarties in her mouth, then crunched them down into fine pieces before swallowing.

Meemaw sat in her rocking chair and carefully took out one of the little pastel candies from her own pack and placed it on her tongue. Tishanna curiously watched as Meemaw closed her eyes and savored the flavor as it gradually dissolved in her mouth. The steady summer breeze crinkled the empty wrapper lying in Tishanna's hand. Looking at it, she couldn't help but wonder if she had done it all wrong.

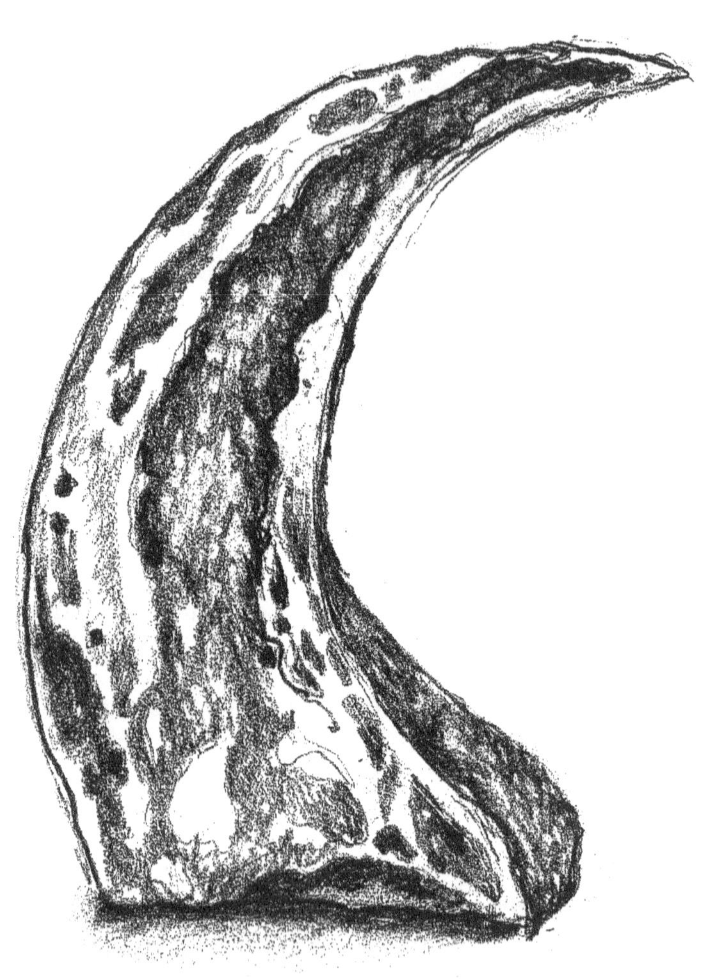

· 7 ·

The Fossil

Soil from the vast desert was brushed away, leaving the fossil well defined; a large claw. The archaeologist carefully picked it up. The fossil felt light but not fragile and retained exquisite detail even after surviving a mass extinction and multiple centuries of burial. Even better, it could easily be dated by the engraving on the bottom of the claw, "Smithsonian 2012, Made in China."

The archaeologist had yet to find this China, but the name brought immense value in the Galactic Black Market. Slithering back to the ship, the archaeologist placed the fossil in his collection of Earthly memorabilia.

· 8 ·

Savor

Coins clink against the glass countertop as the man slides two dollars in change toward the clerk. He takes a plate with a freshly baked brownie and places it in front of the young girl waiting patiently at a table. She reveals her arms from under the large, worn coat draped over her shoulders. The man savors the girl's smile while his stomach rumbles incessantly.

The brownie's warmth thaws her fingers, giving her a sensation as pleasurable as the brownie's taste. The girl keeps each bite small. She needs it to last. For her, this only comes once a year.

· 9 ·

Throw Pillows

Keep the throw pillows on the loveseat!" cried Sheila's grandmother running to shove them all back onto the couch. "The more pillows, the more difficult for the Devil to sit."

Sheila sighed. Home from college, she only wanted to read in peace. Once her grandmother left for the store, Sheila returned to the loveseat, throwing the pillows to the floor. She stretched out, taking comfort in the red velvet and firm armrests. Warm and inviting. She felt something move under her legs. Sheila lowered her book, startled to find a man sitting beside her. He winked and said, "Hey, toots."

· 10 ·

Original Sin

A feather fell from the sky, and the people witnessed it in horror as it floated to the ground and landed in the center of the village. The villagers were quick to gather their children, their elderly, and anyone that made easy prey. Doors were locked, and eyes peeked through shut curtains. Then they waited. And they watched.

A piercing screech sounded and caused the children to whimper. Wings thrashed the air, and the hearts of the women and men raced. The creatures looked like angels–beautiful winged humanoids–but their nature was primeval. They hunted sinners, and no one was safe.

$$\cdot\ 11\ \cdot$$

Hands of Time*

She holds his hand in hers and wonders how something so extraordinary can be so small. Growth is slow, but time is slippery. Years feel like moments to her, and his hand begins to fill her palm, threatening to break their bond.

Fingers continue to extend, and muscles grow stronger, and before she can ready herself for this inevitable change, his hand matches hers in size. She watches her own hand shrink till the skin sags around the bones. His hand begins to overtake. He holds her hand in his and wonders how someone so extraordinary can become so small.

** Originally published in Microfiction Monday Magazine, May 3, 2021*

· 12 ·

Mystery Wig

A wig, now a wet mass of black curls, sits in my backyard. Mud cakes the inside after a heavy rain. What was its journey? Was it tossed from a vehicle and into the wind in a moment of excitement or frustration? Did a large bird snatch it from some poor soul's head for nesting purposes? Maybe the owner is close by, slowly being unearthed from years of erosion of the nearby creek.

However it got here, I wasn't going to let it stay. Using a pair of tongs, I threw it over the fence. Another step in its journey.

· *13* ·

Last Call

"Closing time, boys," said the bar matron to the last two patrons. The usual crowd had dissipated long before the moon reached its peak, as was custom. However, these two were outsiders.

"Aye, darling," said one. "We still got sorrows to drown."

The other walked his fingers up the matron's thigh. "You look scrumptious," he said.

"Funny. I was about to say the same," she grinned. Her muscles bulged, tearing her dress. Then came the fangs and fur. The men struggled. They always did. But their deaths wouldn't be for nothing. The meat lasted the village for the next week.

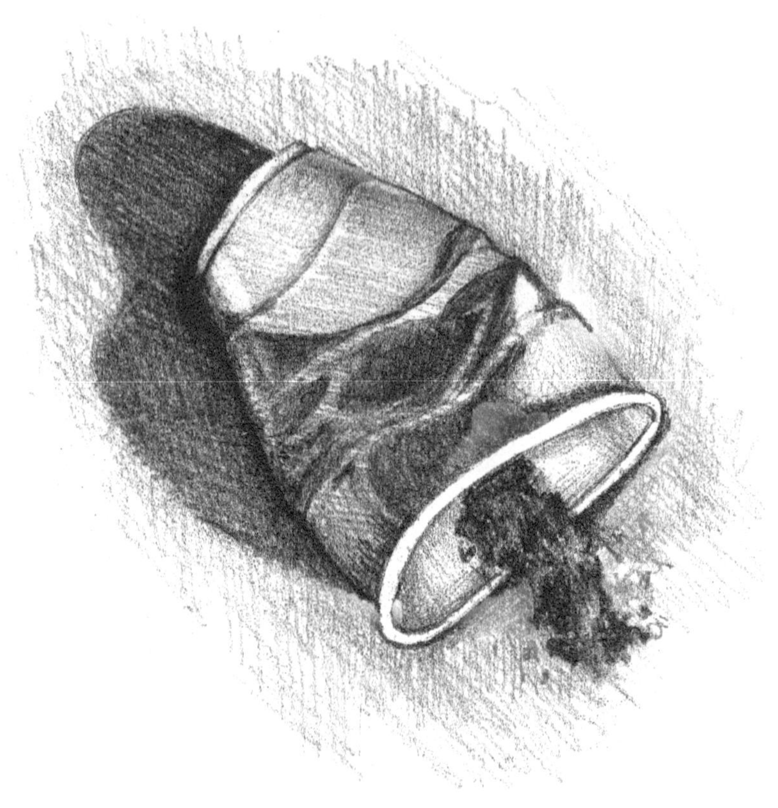

· 14 ·

Last to Leave

Ted walks a red wasteland. He is the last remaining member of the original party. His metallic suit and fishbowl helmet are lightweight, yet still, Ted drags his feet, kicking up dirt like a child scorned. "They all left without me," he thinks aloud. This place is alien to him. If the throbbing in his head wasn't enough, the heat begins to turn his gut inside out.

Ted opens the visor on his helmet, but the air is dry and coarse. "If I make it back to civilization," he swears. "I'll never again go to a desert rave on Halloween."

The Daily Journal

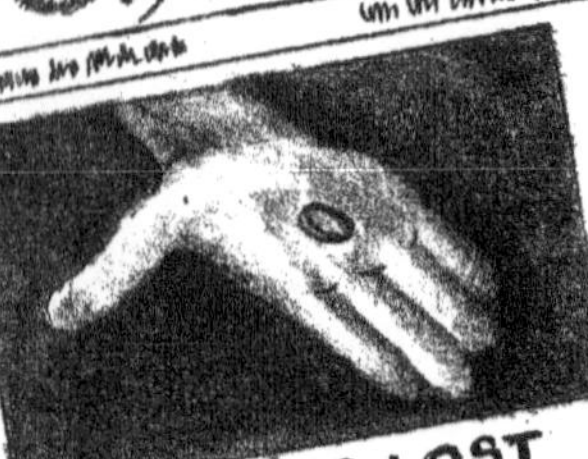

ESCAPED
ORANGUTAN
FINALLY
CAPTURED
MAN FINDS LOST
WEDDING RING
DISMEMBERED
BODY FOUND

· 15 ·

The Body

What should we do with the body?
We'll need to move it.
The space won't be big enough.
Probably need to cut it in half to make it fit. Place the rest somewhere else.
I just don't want it to get too messy. People will be turned off by it.
I've been doing this for years. Trust me, no one will ever notice.
Someone always notices.
It's already past five. I'm going home.
Fine. I will figure something out.
Make sure to get that piece done before we go to the printers. I am not letting another issue release late.

· 16 ·

Guilt

The peppy girl in tight yoga pants sips on her overpriced hot coffee. She says something while scrolling through her phone. The middle-aged man sitting opposite her nods and gives a disinterested groan. He glances at the other patrons sitting around him. His brow furrows. A knot forms in his gut.

Looking at his watch, he has a few hours before his flight. He rubs the indentation in the skin around the base of his ring finger. Gripping his similarly overpriced iced coffee tightly, he lets the cold numb his fingers. "You ready to get outta here?" he then asks.

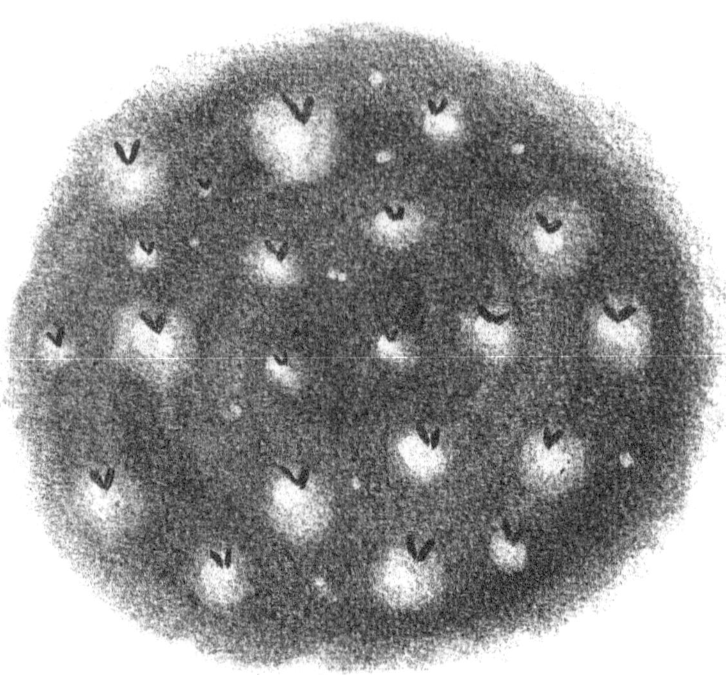

· 17 ·

The Lake

I remember the fireflies and how their light reflected off the dark water. I remember the soft rocking of the boat and the warmth from my father's arms wrapped around me. But that day never happened. Dad died when I was five. He sold the boat before I was born. We never saw the fireflies.

So why, when I go to the lake, does it all come rushing back? I feel wrong for having it. Like it's contraband. Something precious was stolen from another version of myself. One good memory that I never got to live. A gift or curse?

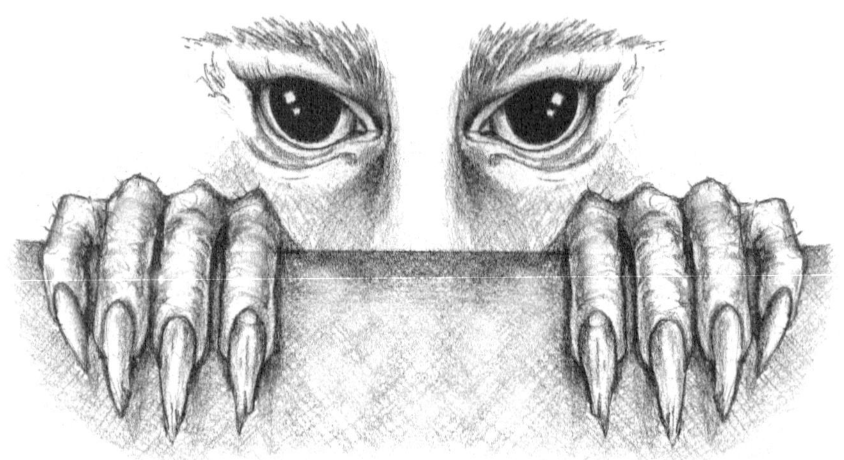

· 18 ·

Hungry Eyes

The babysitter liked to watch horror movies. She forced me to watch them with her. One showed a monster creeping up on some sleeping girl. Hot breath tickled the back of her neck. She turned, opened her eyes. It's crouched at the edge of the bed, claws pinching the sheets and staring with hungry eyes.

After the movie, the babysitter said it was time for bed. In the dark, I sneak back into the living room. The babysitter is asleep on the couch. My hot breath tickles her neck. Then she turns and sees my claws and my hungry eyes.

· 19 ·

Of Thunder and Lightning

Brent's heart beat in unison with the windshield wipers. Sweat greased his palms, and an ale-induced haze plagued his vision. He forced his eyes off the rearview mirror and onto the road. Thunder ravished the sky. Wind tore at the trees and rammed Brent's pickup truck from side to side. Something passed overhead in the darkened sky, and lightning shattered the road forcing Brent to stop suddenly.

From the smoke and debris came another man, tall, muscles swelling under a flannel shirt, with long blonde hair and a thick beard. The man declared, "No mortal will grab my lady's rear!"

· 20 ·

Expecting

Amazing! Intelligent! Special! Gifted! If Kelsey heard one more compliment about her fiancé's nephew, Daniel, she was going to scream or at least shove her fiancé's untouched muffin down his throat. Daniel was only eight, and everyone acted as if he was the greatest life form in the universe.

"Hopefully, it runs in the family," her fiancé said. He reached across the table and slid his hand along the top of Kelsey's, gripping her fingers gently. "I guess we'll see soon."

Kelsey feigned a smile to appease him. His grip tightened on her fingers.

"Right?" he asked.

"Right," Kelsey replied.

· 21 ·

Blossom and Thrive

Thin, dry limbs snapped effortlessly under the gentle force of sharp iron digits. The automaton had worked for decades determining what was weak. And it had done well at removing said weaknesses. Thorns brushed against the groundskeeper's steel shell, creating a piercing screech. A cry similar to the numerous audio files the groundskeeper had recorded from its work in the camps. Those cries eventually died out, and the groundskeeper had found a new use in line with its original purpose. The local municipal rose garden had benefitted beautifully. Cutting out the weak allowed for what remained to blossom and thrive.

· 22 ·

Broken

Happy was a misnomer, as Happy Monahan was the most rotten son-of-a-bitch between New Mexico and Missouri. Happy broke horses good and hard. One day a group of horse thieves approached. Happy took off on his horse, but the bandits were catching up fast. He dug his spurs into the flesh of his ride, but the beast remained at a steady pace. A bullet pierced his back and out his chest. He hit the ground, and his nag came to a stop. As Happy's blood wet the parched earth, he realized he didn't just break horses. He broke their spirits.

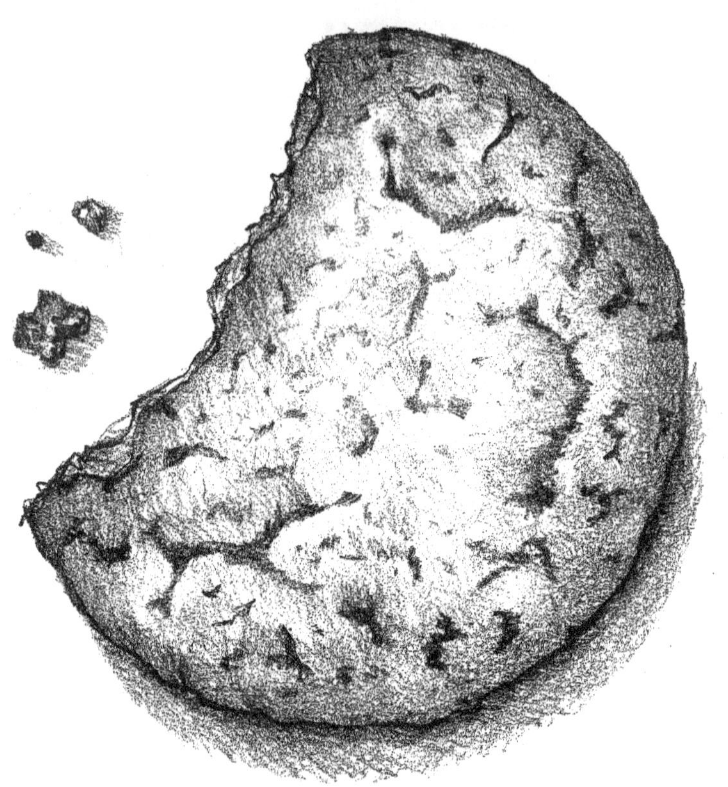

· 23 ·

Normalcy

I feel sick," said Kim returning a half-eaten pumpkin cookie to the nearly empty display case next to the counter.

"Should've started with the sugar-free ones," replied Linda, her hand trembling as she poured the last of the coffee grounds into the machine. Linda enjoyed the noise of freshly brewing coffee. It brought a sense of normalcy. Maybe that is why she still wore her apron and ball cap? Normalcy. For days, they listened to the screams of those still outside. Now, all they heard was the occasional other-worldly howl or moan while indiscernible shadows moved past the barricaded windows.

· 24 ·

Santa's Come to Town

In a dark office, Agent Kris Kringle sits tied to a chair. Surrounding him are Meisterburger and his goons. "You are all going on my Naughty List," says Kringle.

Meisterburger laughs. "Let me start that list for ya." Pulling out a pen and paper, he writes their names down. "Mine's in bold at the top, so you don't forget it." He and all but one of his goons leave. "Kill him," he orders the remaining goon. Quickly, Agent Kringle breaks his bonds and shoves a piece of coal down the goon's throat. He grabs the list. "You better watch out."

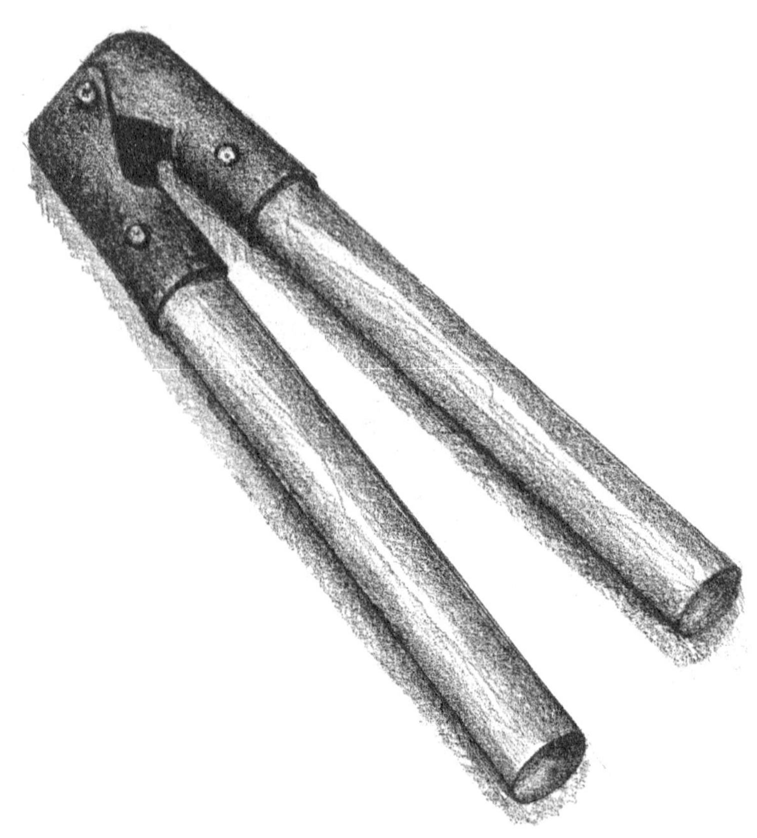

· 25 ·

The Curse

The Asters didn't own cattle, yet had a sizable pair of dehorners in the barn, passed down from generation to generation. Their lineage was wrought in cursed love. Love like that of Pasiphae for the bull. They were blessed with many children who grew brutish. Each sixteenth birthday brought unnatural sounds that permeated the night. Rumors spread. Some local boys got curious. On the eve of an Aster child's sixteenth, the boys traversed the impressive display of corn crops, which hid the Aster home. There, they learned why the family covered their heads and kept their hair bushy and long.

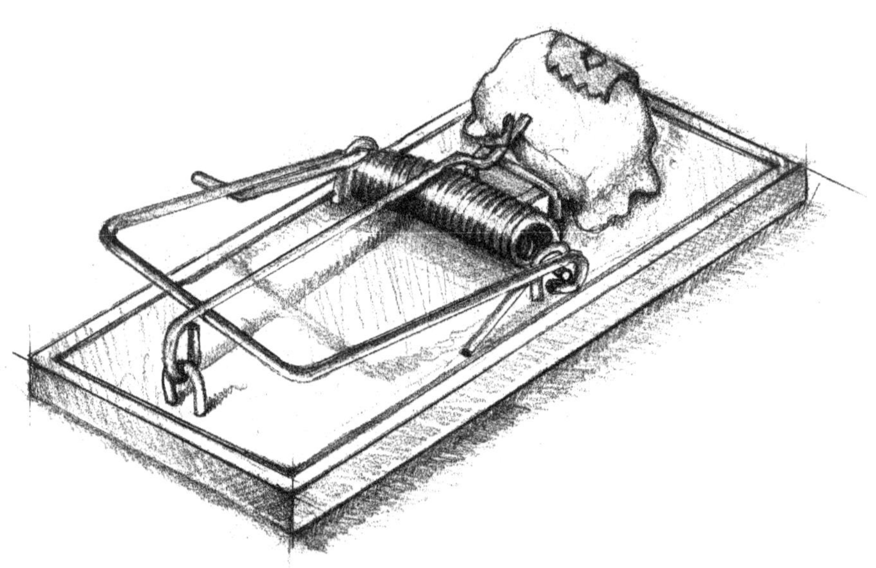

· 26 ·

Pest Control

"Little bastards," said Meredith, placing small traps throughout her attic. A glob of butter set gently upon each spring-loaded device, something her particular pest could not resist. Satisfied by her work, Meredith retired for the evening. The next morning, Meredith awoke with nervous anticipation. Hastily stepping out of bed, she felt something bite her toes. She wailed in pain. One of her traps dangled from her toe. The barbaric devices covered the entire floor of her bedroom. "Winged freaks!" she yelled. Mischievous giggling came from every dark corner of the room, and the buzzing of tiny wings filled Meredith's ears.

· 27 ·

Refuge

Shells blasted the darkening horizon. Felix watched from his post along the wall of Kaltrixia's southern border. War brought refugees. Too many for Kaltrixia to handle, forcing them to shut down the border. Felix served out of a naive sense of duty. Figures climbed the wall, hidden in the flashes of destruction. Felix rushed to the spot and raised his laser rifle. A father tried helping his son down. Felix approached. Fear betrayed the father's otherwise intimidating figure. Lowering his weapon, Felix helped the child. He knew his orders. But seeing where they came from, Felix couldn't send them back.

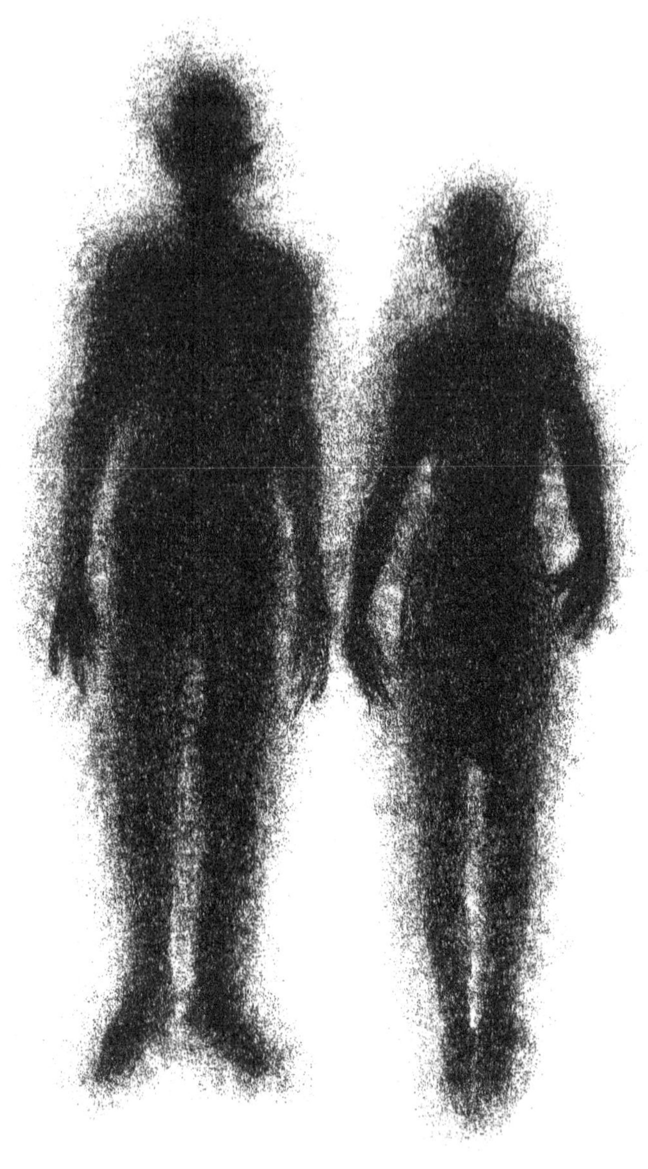

· 28 ·

In His Dreams

In his dreams, he sees monsters. At first, they appear familiar and safe. They smile and lure him into their loving embrace. Then they change. Their fingers and arms turn shadowy and long. Their heads are replaced with horrible things. He can't leave. He feels tied to them. They call him "Son" and profess their love with a bitter aftertaste of venom. They will always be with him. Their faces will sear into his mind, and eventually, when he wakes, there will be no mask they can hide behind. But for now, he will only see monsters in his dreams.

· 29 ·

Unforeseen Consequences

Harry knew every lump, heap, and mound on his property, yet the new debris pile near the woods baffled him. He approached cautiously and examined the strange mass. Sticks and shrubbery appeared almost interwoven like a blanket or tarp.

So Harry got a burning permit, lighter fluid, and matches. He lit the pile. The flames grew. Then the mass shook. Flaming debris flew off, and a hairy, plump, ten-foot-tall troll emerged. The creature fled in pain, crashing through the front garden before being hit with sunlight, turning it instantly to stone. Harry stood in dismay at his new lawn ornament.

· 30 ·

Interlude

An ethereal mist slipped through her fingers as she slipped between life and death. Within the hazy abyss into which she perpetually fell, called the magician's voice. His exaggerated syllables impregnated the air, and the strange humidity of this place between places wet her ears as his hot breath had so many times before. Drifting between existence and nothingness had become an addiction. Here she felt nothing. Time didn't stop but moved like a gentle breeze crisscrossing along the water's surface. Then the master beckoned her to return. One day she wouldn't. But for now, the show must go on.

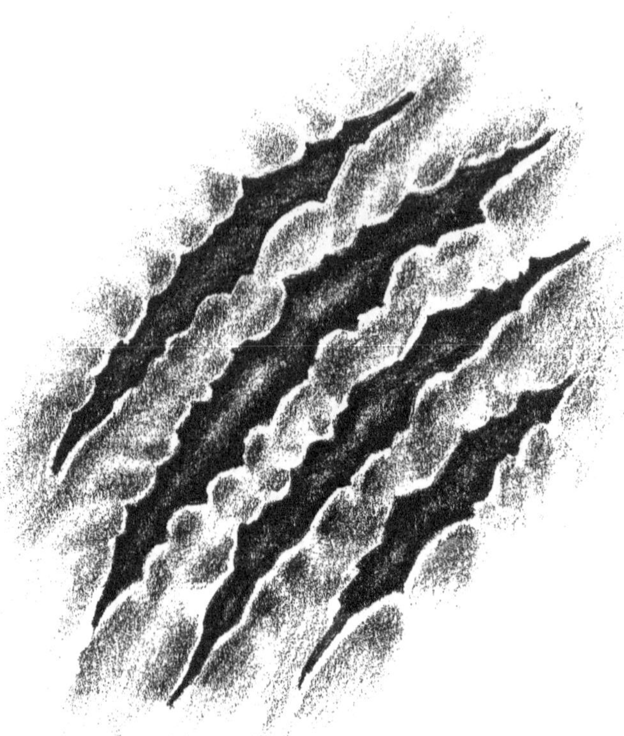

· 31 ·

In Those Moments

They think he's possessed. The family theorizes openly, for he does not speak their language. Perhaps it is something dark and otherworldly that has taken him. He finds amusement only in destruction and chaos. When night approaches, he is closed away in the bathroom so that the rest of the family may rest easy. Attempts at affection are met only with resistance and tantrums. Discipline results in nothing but heightened aggression, cries of frustration, and sometimes blood. Some moments, though fleeting, he rubs up against a leg, arm, or chest and begins to purr. In those moments, they find hope.

· 32 ·

Wandering Altar

The last prayer heard by the altar was for water. Before that, a prayer for fire. Then, for years, there were no prayers. No wants or needs. An order was sent from above: the altar must find new prayers. Breaking hard clay, the altar unearthed itself and traversed charred landscapes on bulky stone limbs. All it found for miles were the crumbs of civilization. Nothing survived whatever wrath had washed over the land. It was the only remaining connection to the ones above. With no prayers, an altar was just stone. And those above had lost all influence and power.

· 33 ·

Rebuild

Mason stood surrounded by 20 years of his family's life splintered and broken. A rapid vortex of wind and debris had ripped through the countryside. His wife and son crept out from the shelter he had built after his first brush with nature's indiscriminate wrath. Mason couldn't help but feel this was becoming personal. This was his second warning. Under his family's tears, he saw their fear and hopelessness. To move would bring uncertainty. He hated the idea of starting over again. The words nearly choked him. But he spits it out. They needed something familiar. "We'll have to rebuild."

· 34 ·

On Fear

Jake puts his cat in a pillowcase and twists the open end closed in his hands. He swings it, careful not to hit anything. He doesn't want to hurt it. "Just scare it is all," he says. "Fear is good. It teaches us not to get too comfortable." Something his dad says. I don't stop him. He's ten, two years older than me. And bigger. The cat cries out. Jake says it is not a big deal. He stops once something pungent drips from the pillowcase. The cat escapes and hides somewhere. From then on, it remains skittish around people.

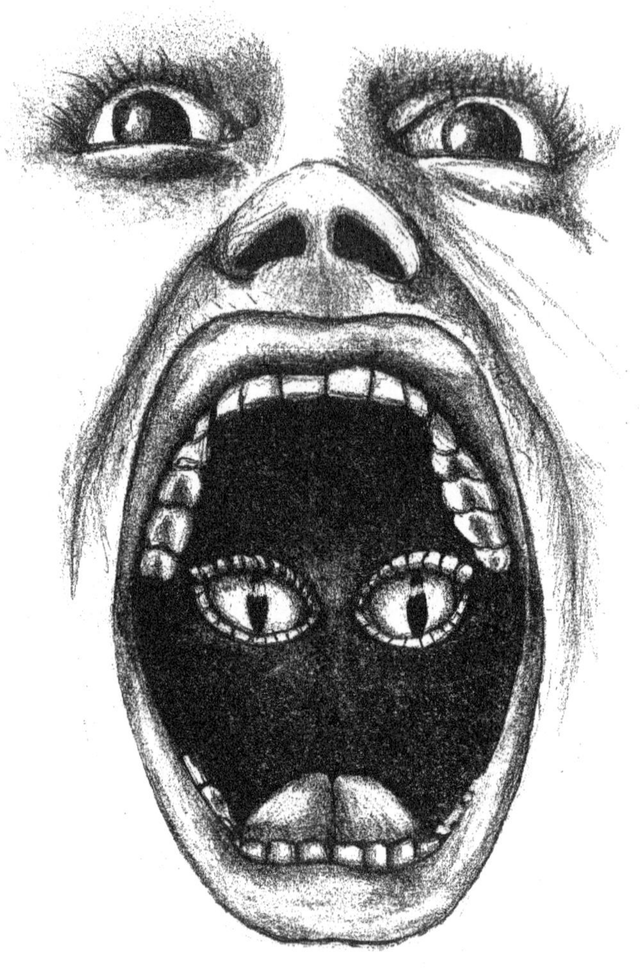

· 35 ·

Infiltration

Bill's arm stopped functioning. A burnt smell wafted from his armpit. Muffled screeching filled his head. Quick action was required, or else the finger he used to press delete threatened to continue erasing the forty-page document his team created. He manipulated joints and mechanisms until both arms shot upward.

"Bill, you took my yoga advice!" said a passing co-worker.

Bill turned and smiled stiffly. Smoke poured into his head. An immediate evacuation was the only option. Bill's mouth opened, allowing a little reptilian creature to escape onto the desk. A new body would need to be constructed for future infiltrations.

· 36 ·

A Real Job

Thirty-year-old Dick Clifford had given up on his life's ambition to become a swordsman. Dick was fully aware that skills in the art of the blade were not a viable source of income, but at least he had tried. His mother was especially thankful as now Dick could find a real job and move out. Countless applications and rejections passed, and then the most remarkable thing happened. A position opened at a year-round medieval theme park. Dick cheered. His mother sighed. Now, he cleans the theme park's restrooms, dreaming of one day donning the brilliant armor of "Royal Gate Attendant."

· 37 ·

Everywhere He Had Been

The purge started with his favorite chair. The faux leather upholstery ripped like paper. Stuffing squished between her fingers. Next, she scrubbed her toilet with his toothbrush, then burned his clothes in the yard with her favorite sheets to cleanse the bedroom of his smell.

Yet, he lingered. She touched her lips and gagged, tempted to drink bleach because he had been there. In the shower, she scrubbed her skin raw because he had been there. She gripped her belly and wanted to tear out her own insides because he had been there. When would he end and she begin?

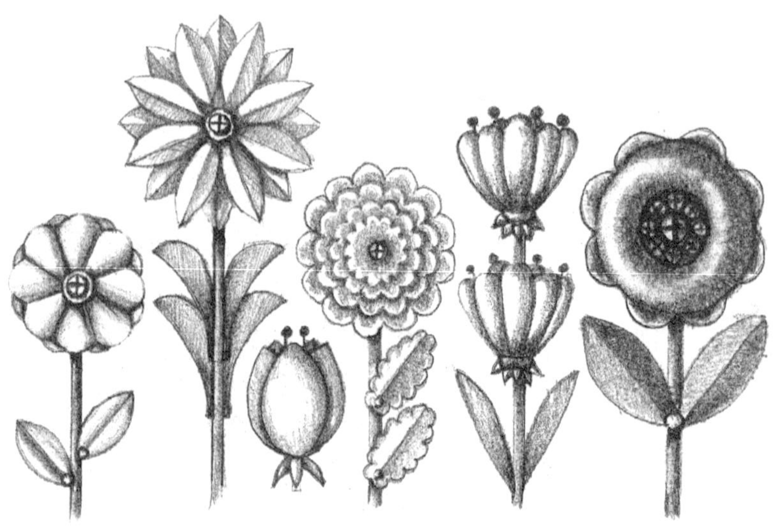

· 38 ·

New Flowers

Withered flowers drooped across Susan's hands. In a fit of rage, she threw them in the air in all directions and cursed the universe and herself for not getting it right again. Her husband saw this from the kitchen and wanted to help. That night, he didn't go home. He stayed in the shop cutting and shaping metal. In a cabinet, he found some old paint and used it the best he could. In the morning, Susan woke up to her husband outside. Metal flowers of all shapes and sizes filled her garden. She had never seen anything more beautiful.

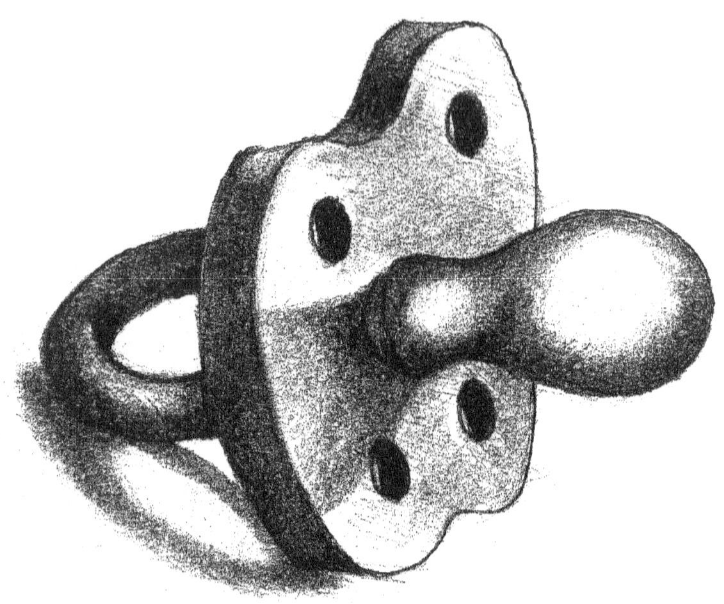

· 39 ·

After Birth

A dozen baby books, eight weeks of Lamaze, and seemingly endless doctor appointments. We were more than prepared for the delivery. After the delivery (and sacrificing the afterbirth to Shishmigoth), we finally got home and fell onto the couch. My wife and I were lost in silence. All that preparation, and we hadn't been prepared for what came after. He had to live at least until he was eighteen before leaving home to devour the cosmos. Add another ten years if he turned out to be a nerdy introvert. Though tough, we would take it one day at a time.

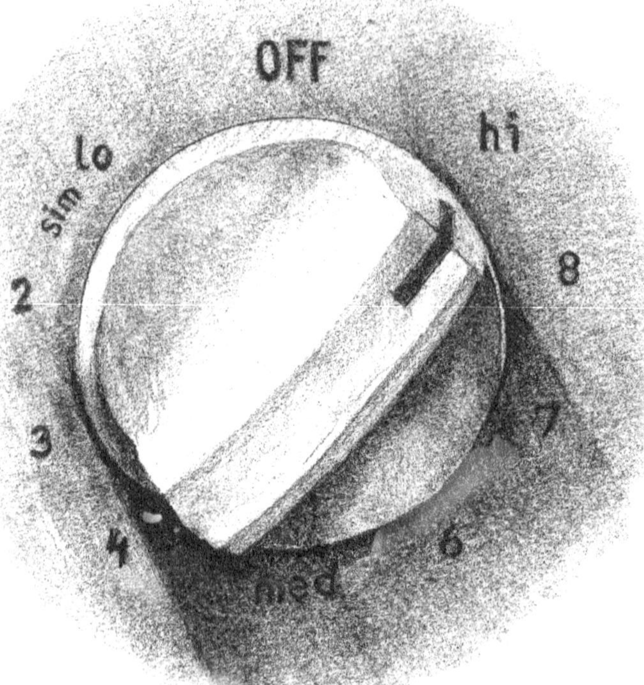

OFF
sim lo
hi
2
8
3
7
4
6
med

· 40 ·

A Spark

It started with a spark. From across the ballroom, I saw the embers dance in the air. Flowing dark chocolate hair paired well with her Cabernet-colored eyes. We kissed behind closed doors. She scoffed and turned away, a warm glow all around her. I followed her to the kitchen. No one was around. She sat on the stove in red stockings, turned the dial on high. I felt the heat rise, and the promise I made melted in my hand. A roaring flame birthed underneath us. While she turned my world to ash, she laughed. And I laughed with her.

· 41 ·

New Toy

The blinking lights and laser sound effects enraptured Billy as he played with his new toy robot. How he got it, he wasn't sure. Then he had that nagging feeling that this was only a dream. He wished to stay longer, but his lucidity had already begun attacking his dreamscape. The morning light of the real world was leaking in. Billy ran to his toy chest and dropped the robot inside. That morning Billy lay awake and replayed the dream in his head. He looked at the chest with a glimmer of hope. To his surprise, the robot was there.

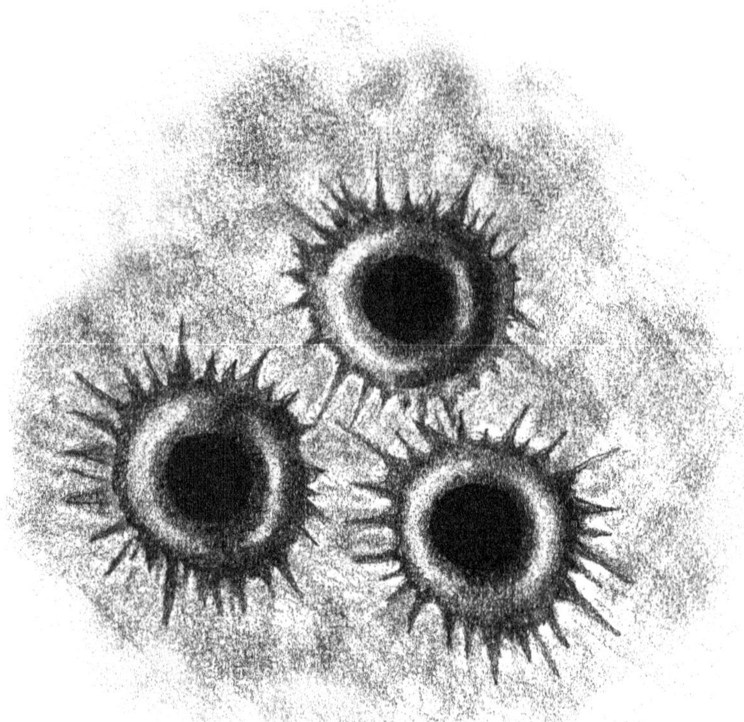

· 42 ·

You Say You Want a Revolution

Amother finds a seat on the transport ship. There are few other riders. She runs a hand through her short messy hair. The once fiery orange has long faded and exposes a natural gray. Ash and dirt spot her lime-colored dress. Something fast and hard hits the ship's roof. No one seems to care. She is tired of this revolution and what it has taken from her. Faces she once knew and supported are unrecognizable. Yet, their promises stay the same. Always the same. She no longer cares who "wins" as long as it ends. Let it all end.

· 43 ·

Closure

His trash bag is burdensome as he stumbles onto the bus. The bag hangs in his hand like a laminated tumor. He's elderly, with clothes that look just as weathered. His ride is short, draping his fingers over the line and letting gravity do the pulling. The bus stops near a cemetery where a funeral is happening. He approaches the open grave, casket laid within. To the shock of the family, he empties the trash bag into the hole. Letters filled with empty promises bury the deceased. Leaving, the man lets the breeze carry the trash bag up and away.

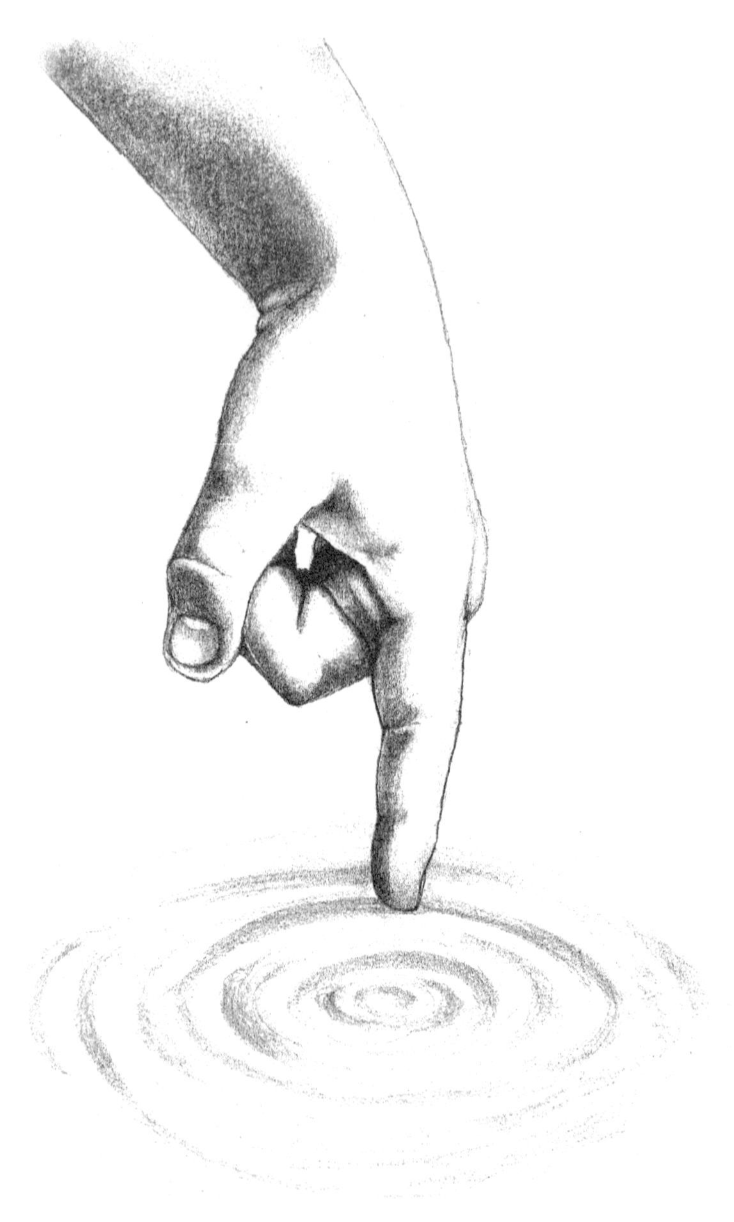

· 44 ·

Playing God*

Kara observed the pond's shore. Subaqueous hills and strange plant life brought new wonders. Kara poked her finger through the yellowish water and planted it in the soft sediment. Tiny creatures scattered in fear. A shockwave of debris blanketed the little world. Enter a new dark age. Kara's reflection appeared in the hazy brown. Was this what it was like to be a god? She quickly removed her finger. The sudden interruption of life wasn't her intention. She never wanted to be feared. Curiosity had gotten the better of her. As the dust settled, life returned, and Kara found relief.

---

* *Originally published in Clover + Bee Magazine, August 28, 2021*

· 45 ·

Make New Ones*

A white discoloration had claimed almost every photo Rahul had taken in the last several years. This disease was born from accidental exposure to light. Vacations, his daughter's wedding, the gorgeous woman that he had been lucky enough to call his wife, had all fallen victim to this partial erasure. As a similar disease ate away at his mind, Rahul cut out what details were left: a mountain range, a brilliant orange marigold, and his love's piercing hazel eyes. Rahul would make new memories with what he had left and hold on to it for as long as he could.

Originally published in Clover + Bee Magazine, August 28, 2021

· 46 ·

He Paints the Dead

He paints the dead, and he paints them well. Each portrait meticulously captures every rotten detail: Blackened flesh hanging off the bone, chipped and blood-stained teeth, eyes lost within an eternal fog. He wants to honestly depict the new world and its people. His portraits hang in malls, museums, subway tunnels, libraries, schools, and little houses tucked away in the woods. They mostly go unnoticed. On occasion, a ghoul stops to observe one of these many pieces. A spark goes off in its shriveled brain. It tilts its head in recognition or puzzlement or understanding. But the moment is fleeting.

HOME
MOVIES

· 47 ·

Stop. Rewind. Play.

All I can do is sit. Sit and stare at the screen as an old home video plays what was once a happy memory. We were just kids living it up in a little motorized jeep. Driving around the cul-de-sac, enjoying the summer breeze. I'm driving as always. Jake is next to me. I hit the curb. It's a funny mistake. Stop. Rewind. Play. I would make that mistake again. When we're older and in my new car. I shouldn't have been driving. Especially after that party. Now Jake is gone, and all I can do is sit. Rewind. Play.

· 48 ·

Perfect Union

Yuna barely tolerated drives through the countryside and the lonely hills. Her husband didn't seem to notice. From behind the hills came a murmuration. The black mass of birds twisted and flowed in magnificent shapes. She admired their connectedness and ability to move and change at a moment's notice as if they were a perfect union. With the top down, Yuna leaped from the vehicle to join the little creatures that seemed to have it all figured out. Yuna's flight was momentary before crashing into the roadside brush. The car faded into the distance; her husband oblivious to her escape.

· 49 ·

Power of Love

He marches to their cheers and applause. Tears run from red puffy eyes in a sea of beige uniforms. The people convulse with violent emotion at the sight of their magnificent leader. Some faint, while others pray that their fingertips will be graced with the slightest touch against his exceptional attire. The leader observes his procession of tanks and artillery. He thinks, "If this is their love now, what will they do when I die?" He imagines each of his enemies suffering the despair of his people. For the first time, he feels fear over the power he has obtained.

NINA

· 50 ·

Transformation

New year, new me. It was a common sentiment that people brought into the New Year, yet so few would actually achieve any sense of change. Nina was one of the many who continually failed to keep her goals: intensive workout routines, restrictive diets, unrealistic travel goals, unused watercolor paints, and a half-finished outline for a book. She should've won an award for how often she failed. But this year would be different. After waking up in the body of her 25-pound chocolate Labradoodle, Poochy, Nina cursed the one time she dabbled in witchcraft for a quick body transformation spell.

IDAHO
WISCONSIN
MISSOURI
OREGON
MINNESOTA
MICHIGAN
COLORADO
NEVADA
NEW MEXICO
NEW YORK
OHIO

· 51 ·

Bucket List

The cancer had done a number on Gary, but it wouldn't stop him from his goal. Within a year, the spirited forty-something traveled to all fifty states. From the ridged white-capped mountains of Montana to the beautiful beaches of Hawaii. From the desert of Arizona to the bustling metropolis of New York. He saw the sites and listened to the people. Gary had no regrets about lying on his deathbed in the hospital. Then the nurse turned on the TV to show him the incredible news. "Puerto Rico is officially the 51st State." With his dying breath, Gary whimpered, "Fuuuc…"

· 52 ·

Trick or Treat

Pink, lumpy cake squished between the man's rotting fingers. In an infantile manner, he mashed the dessert into his mouth. He groaned, allowing the cake to fall from his lipless face and onto the plate. The cronish woman sitting across from him erupted into a piercing cackle that echoed throughout the empty cafe and into the night air. "Told you it wasn't real brains!" She took a sip of her steaming coffee and immediately spat it out, partially spraying her undead acolyte. He groaned.

"Take this away!" she hissed at the bewitched barista standing beside them. "Witch's brew, my ass."

TEA

· 53 ·

Promises

Well, I didn't think this would actually happen," says Liz. She sighs and looks at the happy couples seated throughout the restaurant. Seated across the table, Anne stares at her tea, stirring the bag inside the cup.

"Twenty years, and we're still single."

Liz looks at Anne, content, "At least we still have each other."

"Does this count as our anniversary?" asks Anne jokingly.

Liz laughs, "We did promise to marry each other. I say that counts." Liz reaches out and touches Anne's hand, stopping her from stirring. "Do you?"

Anne takes Liz's hand, looks up, and smiles. "I do."

· 54 ·

Buried

The ground was soft that night. The shovel Hanna had stolen from her neighbor's shed pierced the dirt as smoothly as her knife had slit his little dog's throat. No more yapping and stepping in shit. The old geezer had been warned. The other neighbors had left town after their child went missing. Too many bad memories. The woods behind the three houses proved the best place to hide the dog's body. A few feet down and Hanna struck something; the neighbor's kid wrapped in plastic. A chill slid down her spine. Then something moved through the bushes. Or someone.

· 55 ·

On the Job

The fire started when Jerry neglected to watch the large furnace at the back of the manufacturing plant. He stared into the flames for over two hours, thinking about his wife sleeping with his brother. Their naked bodies were intertwined on the couch. His couch. The one he bought after getting this job. Before he and the rest of the employees knew it, the flames had grown and started to spread. Fortunately, the plant was saved and without injury. But Jerry lost his job, and the irony of a fire extinguisher plant almost burning down made headlines across the country.

· 56 ·

Negotiation

Monroe checks his watch, 11:55. Thirty minutes had passed, and the man reading the paper two tables down hadn't flipped the page. Across the street, another man sweeps a spotless sidewalk. The waitress brings Monroe a fresh cup of coffee. Her earpiece sticks out as she turns away. He takes a sip. The tightly packed buildings and alleys should create a claustrophobic maze. He dabs sweat from his forehead with a napkin. An older gentleman slips into the seat across from Monroe. His sunglasses hide the pain in his eyes, but not in his voice, "What've you done with her?"

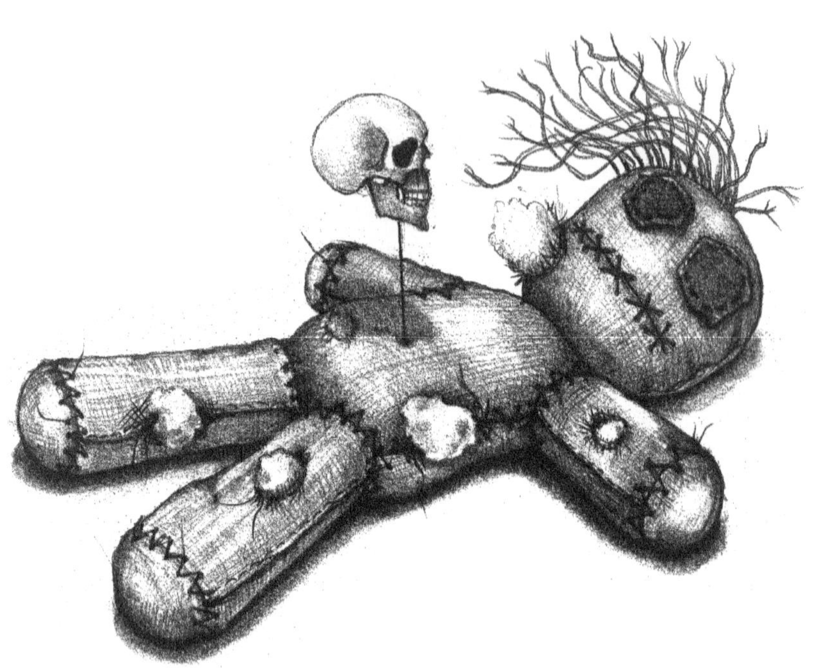

· 57 ·

Stuff

At the bottom of a dumpster was a burlap doll resembling a boy's crude attempt at self-portrait, with green felt eyes and an unevenly affixed bundle of black hair. White stuff protruded from holes across its body. Through its chest was a skull-tipped sewing needle. A young woman shut the window of her studio apartment after tossing the doll. She had no use for it anymore, but she had made a fatal error in her craftsmanship. Her spell claimed the intended victim, and yet... he lingered. The doll removed the needle and imagined what stuff would come out of her.

· 58 ·

Stale

The wine somehow tasted stale. Carol peered into the rich red that filled her glass, searching for a reason. A reason for its staleness. A reason for the foul taste in her mouth. Charlie's glass was empty. Swallowed it all in a matter of seconds. He could taste it too, but he pretended the sweetness had remained. Now he sat on the edge of the bed, unbuttoning his shirt in anticipation of something. Carol eyed the door to their motel room. Then she tipped her glass, and the stale red slipped inside her, and its taste stuck to her throat.

· 59 ·

Chaos Monkey

Humans looked like fat idiots. Bubba watched them from the top of his cage and took a bite of a mushy persimmon. But the bigger idiots were Bubba's clan of black macaques. How could they laugh and grow fat while imprisoned? Then a young human with big spiked hair made terrible noises and gestured wildly. The other humans stopped and looked annoyed. Something about this human and its ability to upset the balance, albeit momentarily, inspired Bubba. Using persimmon mush, Bubba spiked the long patch of fur on top of his head. A menacing smirk stretched across his long face.

· 60 ·

Dinner Guest

All Douglas wanted was to finish his filet mignon, but the intruder brandishing a gun had interfered. The intruder stared at the piece of meat. "Where is it?" she snapped. Douglas kept calm and pointed toward the door leading to the basement. The intruder motioned him forward, so Douglas complied. In the basement's low light sat a single large freezer. The intruder opened it, revealing several cuts of meat carefully packaged and labeled: thigh, ribs, arm.

"He was my partner," she said and turned to fire, but Douglas was quick and incapacitated her.

"If it's any consolation, I've had better."

· 61 ·

Wind and Sunshine

All I gots left is wind and sunshine," said Gram as she clipped the last of the laundry to the clothesline in the backyard. After years of pressure from her family, she conceded to getting a washing machine. But no dryer. She needed something in her life to remain. Everything changed too quickly and with little to no warning. Friends passed, and her small town got smaller. Winters were tough, but she knew the sun would return. In her final moment following a stroke, she lay under the clothesline. The sun's warmth hugged her, and the wind kissed her cheek.

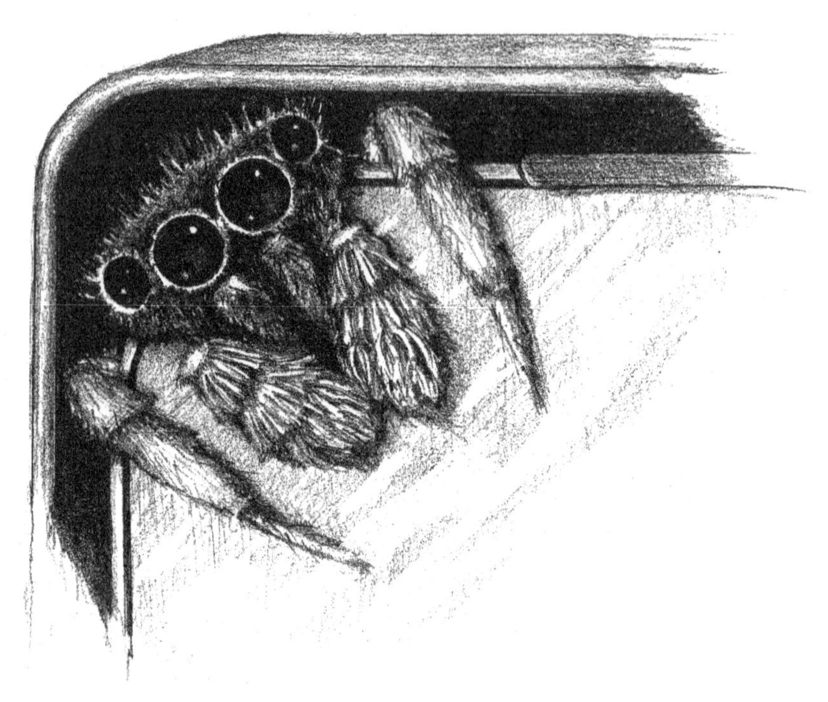

· 62 ·

Whole New World

Hitchhikers come in all types. Some are often quite small with eight legs and covered in hair. Federico fell into this category as perfectly as he had fallen from his web and onto the side mirror of a large truck. Feeling a sudden rumble, Federico hid behind the reflective glass. He traveled from city to city, uncertain of where he would find himself next. Each extended stop allowed him to spin a quick web to catch his next meal. The cuisine! Federico had never seen nor tasted the likes of these insects. He decided then, the world was his home.

· 63 ·

Inheritance

My buzz nearly wore off, pulling into the driveway. Darla sat on the porch, skunky smoke fading from her lips. Neither of us spoke, only nodded. Our father had a message, one that would decide our future. Entering the Victorian home from our youth, we found Father sitting in front of the TV, scotch in hand. Darla placed her hand on his shoulder. I was hesitant to do the same. His mouth opened, and we knew what he would say. "I'm taking you out of the will." We found a burial place later that day. Someplace no one would discover.

· 64 ·

The Adventurer

Vergil was quite the triumphant adventurer. No one in the realm had accrued an extensive collection of treasures as he. Each trinket that adorned his lavish home had an elaborate story to tell. Some more believable than others. Hungry dragons, vicious trolls, disgruntled wizards, he had slain them all. Once a month, Vergil traveled to a cottage nestled deep in the forest. He knocked on the door. A beastly man invited him in. While conversing over tea, the beastly man told Vergil of his adventures and even gave Vergil trophies as the beastly man didn't care for such garish things.

· 65 ·

Disconnected

A warrior and a druid sit at a small table at the back of an inn. They joke with brief pauses in between. The druid says, "You're cool. Name?" The warrior focuses heavily on the word cool. A nervous tremble befalls the warrior's hands, causing a stumbling of words. "Yuor cool too. Im'-" Before the warrior can finish, the world turns black. A text box appears, reading 'You have been disconnected from the server.' A girl sitting at the back of a library in a small town shouts, "Shit!" She pulls off her headphones in frustration. Everyone stares at her.

· 66 ·

The Enemy of My Enemy

Perched high in a pecan tree, the squirrels eyed their foe,—a cat. The dog had grown old and complacent. This new death dealer was spry, getting into a couple good scraps with the natives. How could the squirrels continue harvesting all of the valuable pecans for themselves with a ferocious beast lurking below? Well, they found their own ferocious beast. One that fell from the sky. With red leathery skin, a spiraling mouth of fangs, and a lumpy tail as hard as a rock. The next time the cat was let out, he stayed on the porch with the dog.

· 67 ·

A Rose in the Snow

She has yearned for this day all year. Light hits the snow creating a blinding white desert. The rich visual array of flora is hidden, allowing her to focus on what's important. She walks this new world, a world without complexity. Her mind slips into a calm, gliding through the fresh powdery precipitation. The minor ringing that follows tranquility tickles her ear. She doesn't mind the cold. It deepens her appreciation for the warmth she does feel. She glows like a brilliant rose torch. Every second is cherished before this world melts away. She will make this moment a memory.

· 68 ·

Be Assured

The sign to a small rural church read: "Be assured of Heaven soon." Soon? Molly thought as she drove past. The next week, the sign read: "Have you washed your hands... of sin?" And the week after that: "HE knows what you did." Molly's palms grew clammy. She was sure no one had seen. The growing specificity of the signs kept her up that night. The following Sunday morning, Molly pulled up to the church and went inside. Maybe she would be forgiven for her occasional laziness. From now on, Molly would always wash her hands after using the restroom.

· 69 ·

Held Back

It was over. Gloria had missed her chance. The question, "In season two of The Office, how did Michael Scott injure his foot?" bounced around her brain in the radio DJ's obnoxious whine. "So much for paying off my medical bills," Gloria thought. "Damn spontaneous radio trivia!" If only she hadn't brushed up against a kitchen drawer trying to reach her phone on the opposite counter, the knob catching a belt loop in her pants, yanking her back. After a few moments of self-pity, Gloria spent the rest of the day removing every waist-high handle and knob in the apartment.

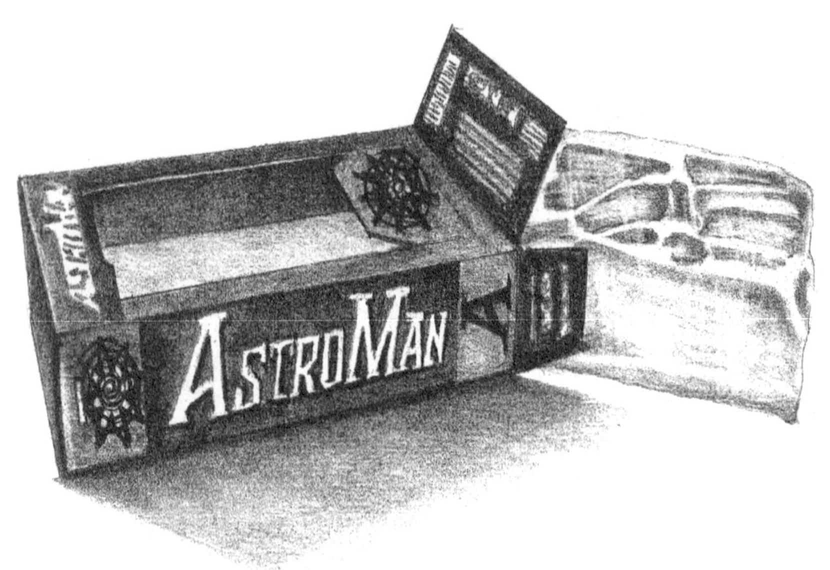
AstroMan
AstroMan
AstroMan

· 70 ·

Mint Condition

Nate's world was made of plastic and cardboard. Most of his fifty years were spent observing his vast collection of action figures. He refused to open even one piece and allow them to suffer the wear and tear of life. Here, they would remain perfect, as if no time had passed. Nate stared into the spotless plastic packaging and reminisced. Sometimes he would catch a glimpse of someone reflected within the transparent casing. A withering husk no better than the fragile encasements he forced upon his inanimate congregation. A cruel reminder of who he is and what he had lost.

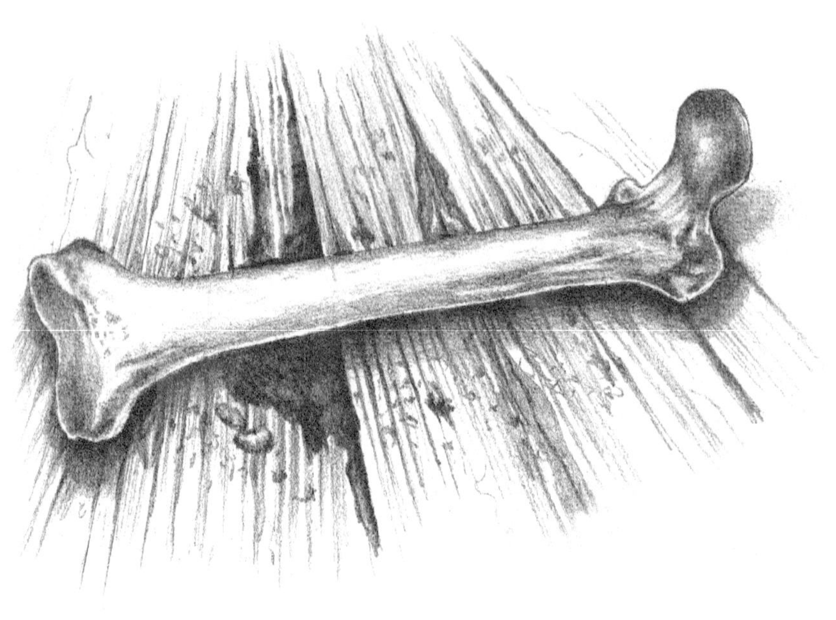

· 71 ·

Siren Song

Thomas drunkenly ventured home through the forest. A woman's voice sang to him in a wonderful melody. He hadn't touched a woman in so long. It pulled him to an abandoned house. Overgrowth of ivy framed an open window radiating orange light on the second story. He climbed the ivy to the window to get a peek. The singing had stopped. The bedroom was cozy. No one was there. He climbed into the room. The light went out. A chill took him. Something crunched under his feet. Bones! Human bones! Frightened, he turned back, but it was already too late.

· 72 ·

Against All Probability

In the maternity ward of a small hospital in Maine, Sarah was screaming her bloody head off. Everything considered, the birth was going quite well. Coincidently, Sally was giving birth in the next room, which confused the hospital staff as she was identical to Sarah in every way. Two healthy baby boys later, the staff was even more perplexed as they too were identical. Sarah met Sally, and the two instantly knew they must be twins separated at birth. When questioned about the father, they gave the same answer: a one-night stand. Against all probability, it was the same man.

· 73 ·

Night Moves

The window had been opened just enough to let in the cool night air. We worked quickly to get things packed up and put into the truck. "Move it. Mom and Dad are almost ready," said my brother as he passed by, carrying the TV. Grabbing the last box, I noticed a blue teddy bear under the bed. Memories flooded back of dragging Dad through the toy store and playing with the same bear before an employee noticed us. No chance of passing this up, I grabbed the bear and headed to the truck. The homeowners would be back soon.

· 74 ·

Animal Man

His clucks were reminiscent of a chicken, and he played the part well: arms flapping and head bobbing, all the while strutting around the outskirts of the Capitol building. Fred often transformed into some creature for theatrical display. He would baa and bark and hiss and hee-haw. Even oink. Anything to get his message across. In college, Fred's biting political commentary and public theatre won him praise from his peers, "You're killing it!", "You're an animal, man!" Thirty years later, tourists cautiously distance themselves from Fred. Meanwhile, the locals laugh and say, "Don't mind him. He's just the animal man."

· 75 ·

Patience

He will come down when he gets hungry. Be patient," Daniel's mother had said. So Daniel tried being patient and discovered he was pretty good at it, occasionally checking to see if the stray cat he affectionately called, Monkey had left the oak tree in the backyard. And then a year passed, and Daniel visited home for winter break. He stepped into the backyard to observe the gray clouds and the oak tree, now stripped of life. Lying on a high branch was a pile of small bones in the shape of a cat. Maybe Daniel had been too patient.

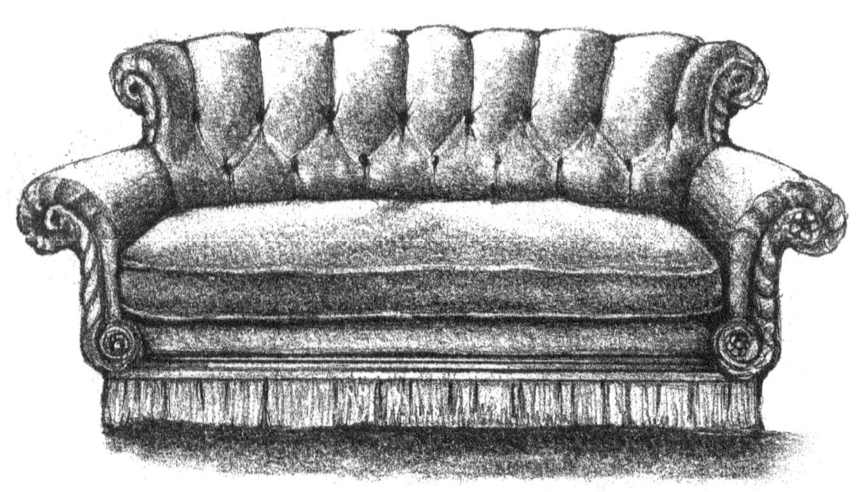

· 76 ·

Friends

Marie sighs and places her book on the table. No use reading, not with that loud group of friends talking in the middle of the coffee house. At least a few of them are there every day and somehow always get the couch and comfy chairs. Marie opens her book but can't help but give the group her undivided attention. The tall one rambles on about his recent divorce. The waitress sits with them, ignoring her duties. She won't get fired. The manager is clearly obsessed with her. The sarcastic guy makes a corny joke. Marie lets a smile slip.

· 77 ·

Chill Pill

You swallow the slender blue capsule and chase it with a shot of whiskey. It was doctor-approved. You even saw his medical license buried in a drawer under the half-empty bottle. A few minutes pass. You count every second. It's gonna be fine. One cold punch to the gut and a chill spreads through your body. Time flies by about 200 years. You're in a lab now with other chill people. The experiment went well, except for the still being consciousness part. You know. You counted every second. Gonna need something a lot stronger to remedy that side effect, huh?

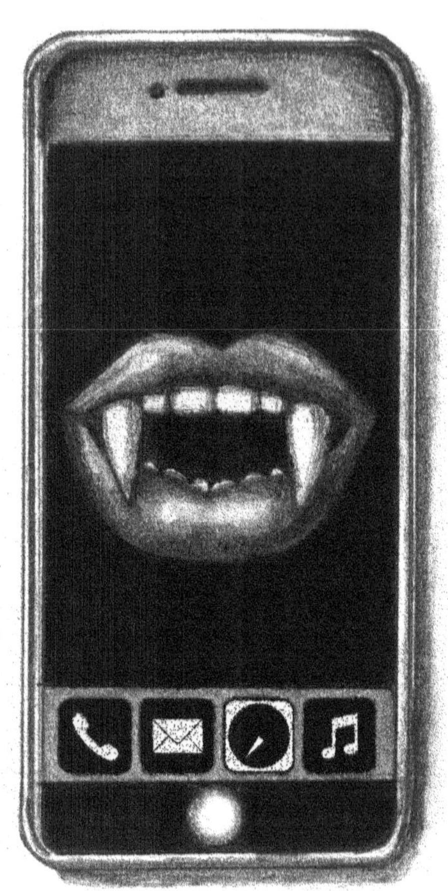

· 78 ·

Red Flags

I'm a late sleeper with a penchant for midnight snacking. Morning people need not apply! Don't try to debate me about history. I'll win. My life's soundtrack is Tito & Tarantula's "After Dark" on loop. I look my best in red. God did me dirty, so don't try and convert me. In other words: start swiping, Jesus freaks! Meet me at the club, and I'll take you to the alley behind it. Pamper me, and I will make sure you're properly rewarded. Looking for someone who isn't afraid of a little rough play in the bedroom. Spoiler: I bite.

Sorry WE'RE
CLOSED

· 79 ·

Uncertainty

Everyone went home, taking their stories with them. The streets were quiet, though the sun was still high. Dust began its gradual, imperceptible drizzle, coating every surface of the cafe. The natural cold had returned to the ceramic mugs stacked under the counter. The rich scent of coffee grounds lingers in the air but will dissipate with time. Wooden chairs were reprieved from the varied and ever-shifting weights of patrons. No keyboard clatter or background chatter or the melody of indie-folk bands and instrumental covers of famous pop songs. This well had been left to dry, leaving a future uncertain.

· 80 ·

Lost to the Void

Regina scours her bedroom for a silver crescent moon earring, a final gift from her late mother. A slip of her fingers and suddenly it was lost. Regina never even heard it hit the floor. She pulls every piece of furniture away from the walls but finds nothing.

Forty years earlier, a young woman sits in the same room, thinking of her future. She hears a clink and finds an earring on the floor. Though not a pair, she keeps it in hopes that one day she will find the other. When she does, it will make a perfect gift.

· 81 ·

At the End of the World

Javier wished for the apocalypse. It would be more exciting than his mechanic job. He had it all planned; a map of locations to scavenge, a fully stocked backpack, and a pistol. He thought survival would make him more confident. Maybe he would help a woman in distress and fall in love. Maybe he would even find himself a good dog.

Then one day, he helped a woman with a flat tire. They talked and dated and fell in love. They even got a dog. Javier was happy and confident. So when the apocalypse did start, he wished it hadn't.

· 82 ·

The Apprentice

His tongue had been taken first as a lesson in not being heard. Next was his left hand in a demonstration of the apprentice's poor defensive form. Each failure cost him more and more until, finally, his master had taken too much. Seeing no more use for him, the master tossed the mangled protege into the streets to live out the rest of his days in shame. But the student's resilience had been callously overlooked. The apprentice would prove his worth as a great and silent warrior, even if it meant killing his old master's other students one by one.

BB
Bill's
BEETLES
AUTO SALES

· 83 ·

No Punch Back

A fist flew, and a child's scream rang out. "Punch buggy red!" said Jenny. Her younger brother, Kyle, rubbed his arm and desperately searched the street for a chance at vengeance.

"Cut it out, guys," yelled their mom from the driver's seat. Every car ride followed the same pattern of violence and censure. That is until an unfortunately specific dealership opened up in town. No one would be prepared for the brutalization that was to come.

"Punch buggy! Red! Blue! Black! Green!" As the dealership faded in the distance, Jenny and Kyle had certainly had their fill of the game.

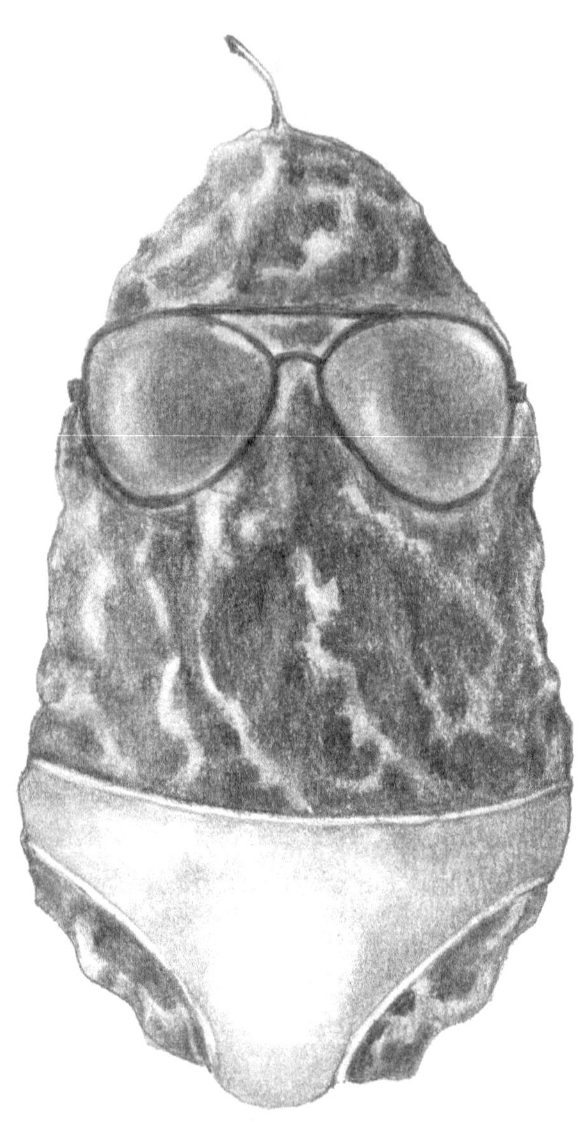

· 84 ·

Sun-Dried Ego

The old man's hand raises, and his arm slightly bends. From the right perspective, it looks like he is holding the sun. The same sun that has browned his skin like a dehydrated sausage. One more, he tells the two bikini-clad girls, whom he has persuaded to take his picture. Try as they might, the girls cannot stop from glancing at the black G-string covering his privates. Then he thanks them for their time and walks the beach proud, thinking he has given them something wonderful. One of the girls giggles. The other hastily deletes the pictures from her phone.

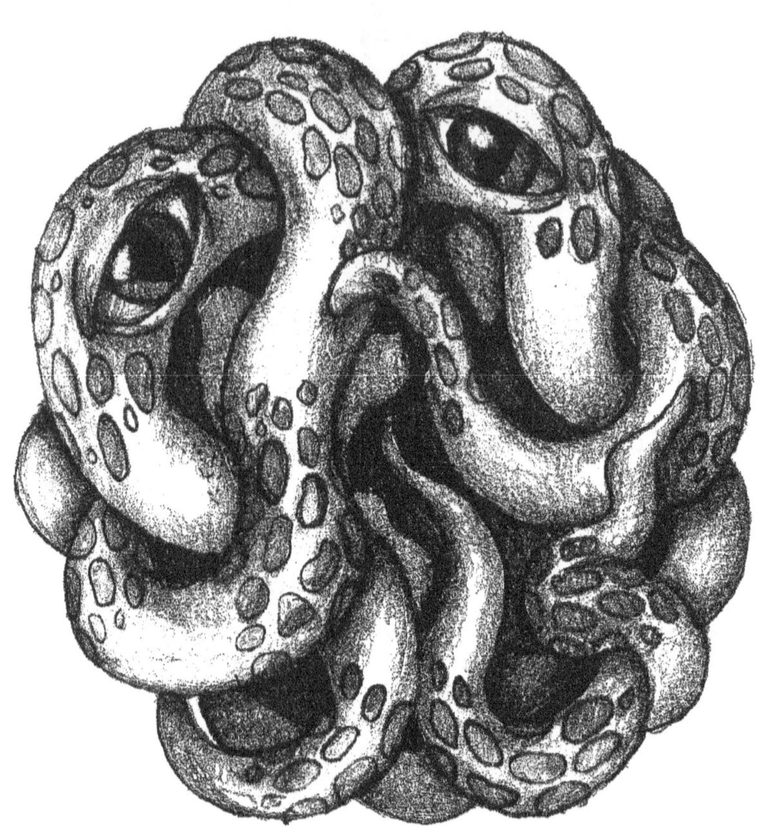

· 85 ·

Under Shadow

We live in the shadow of something else. When it arrived, its many limbs stretched out across our planet and pulled us in. Nothing grows due to the lack of sunlight, and most animals fall victim to human desperation to survive. Our only light comes from its body, glowing in wondrous colors we never thought imaginable. We use the light to burrow into its slimy flesh like maggots to eat its meat and build our new homes. Some theorize that it is eating our planet's core. And most believe it. The only warmth we feel now is from the creature.

· 86 ·

Boston Molassacre

The temperature had climbed too high and too fast, causing the tank holding 2.3 million gallons of molasses to burst. Residents heard a sound like clapping thunder and then a roar. Nearly thirty feet in height, the deep black wave destroyed indiscriminately. Supports snapped like twigs, and buildings crumbled. It sped through the town like a runaway train. Any poor soul caught by the sticky tide was pulled into its depths, seemingly trapped forever like an insect in sap. For decades, survivors were reminded of that horrible day whenever the heat released a familiar sweet smell from the city streets.

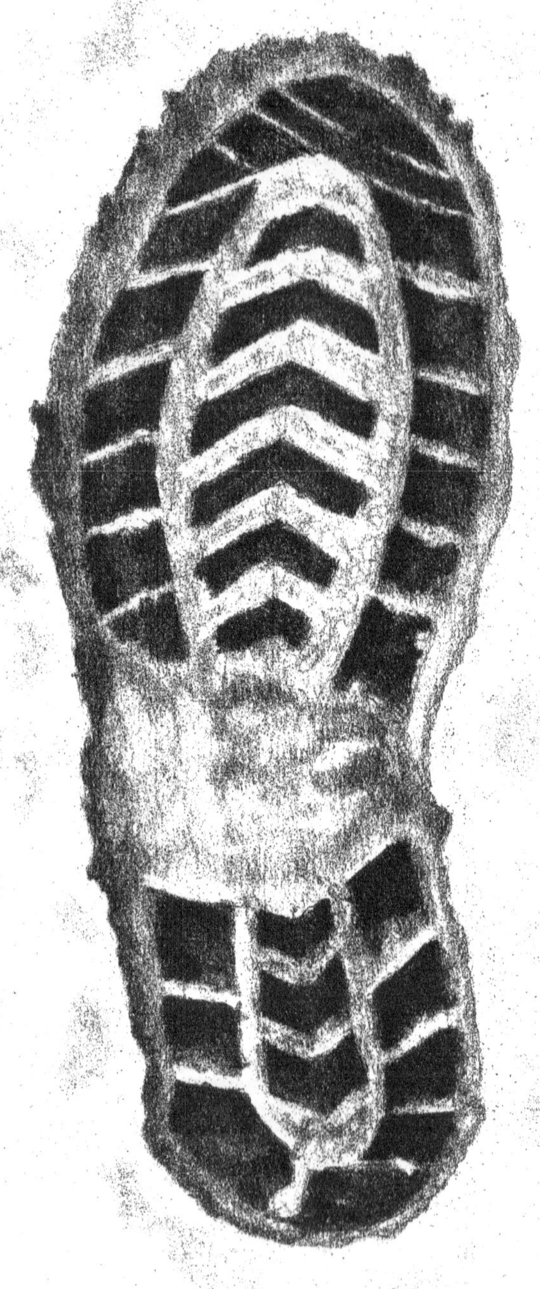

· 87 ·

Good Men

Good men keep their word. Even through snow that suffocated every living thing. He walked for miles. I followed. He often peered back, hoping I was gone or that I had keeled over. Left the bastard disappointed every time. Was he thinking of my girl? Did he think of her at all after he was done? When he cleaned the blood from his hands? He then fell and sunk into the snow, gasping for air that wasn't cold. I stood by his side and watched the light leave him. Just like I said I would. Good men keep their word.

· **88** ·

Late-Night Intruder

His clothes smelled of sweet cinnamon. Moving the sweaters aside, I peered through the slats in the closet door. Lucas, neighbor, and man of my affection, was already in bed, fidgeting in hopes of finding the optimal position. He would find stillness once I was through with him. Then, a blinding light pierced through the curtains, and Lucas froze. The house shook. I blinked, and two disgusting reptilian humanoids appeared standing over Lucas. To my horror, they grabbed him. My Lucas! I burst out of the closet, knife in hand. They never saw me coming, and I got my man.

· 89 ·

Value

After months of research and numerous failed eBay listings, Ron realized his 90's baseball card collection was worth diddly squat. Thanks, increased factory production. Even local charities refused to take his collection. Ron eyed the trash can, then back to his cards. Memories flooded back of cheering with his brother at the TV, watching Ripken's pass over Gehrig's game streak and McGwire's home run record break. Sure, some players were roided up like the Hulk, but the emotion meant more to Ron. Maybe he would keep the cards. What they lacked in monetary value, they made up for in memories.

· 90 ·

A Pirate's Gift

Ninety feet down, lies my gift to any soul," read the lost message of a long-dead pirate. The first fool enraptured by these words found the alleged resting spot and dug until his shovel broke. Only twenty feet. Then he enlisted the help of a friend. Thirty feet more. Then water poured in from beneath the earth and flooded them out. So they came back with more men and better tools. Even machinery to help drain the water. Forty feet more. Then they struck something large and made of iron. A great chest with a note, "I gift you regret."

· 91 ·

Queen of Queens

Applause erupts as the Queen of Queens leads a procession of her kinfolk through the city streets. Each lady shimmers in their own way. They dance and throw up their hands, creating fabulous bursts of confetti. A river of blue silk flows behind the Queen's waterfall figure. The paint around her eyes captures a sky's violet sunrise. Her hair has blossomed into something beautiful. The Queen finds power in this day. It shows in her strut. A boy watches from a low window, mesmerized by a sight he doesn't fully understand. But he wants the freedom that their transformation brings.

· 92 ·

Regret

It feels real. The Commander recognizes the room. The patrons' blurred faces produce a muffled chatter. The rich scent of brewing coffee permeates the air– it smells like home. "You sure it's safe?" asks his wife from across the table. She is perfect, as always.

"No," he wished he'd said. His spacesuit is tattered and hangs on his weary body.

Sunlight accents the fear and wonder in her eyes. "Whaddya think it is, up there?"

"Hell." Outside is dark and cold.

"I know I can't talk you out of this."

He laughs and ends in a dry cough. "I'm sorry."

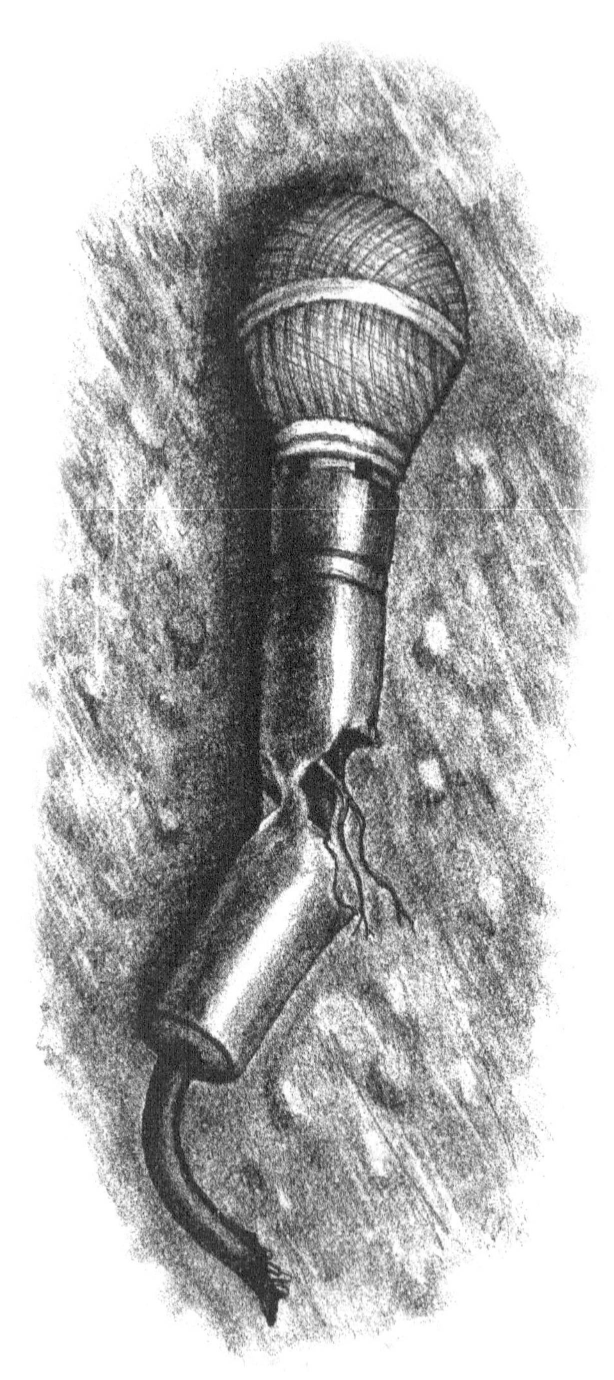

· 93 ·

Comeback Tour

Once upon a time, there was a new artist with immeasurable talent. Fans flocked to show their love and admiration for her. With time, the artist was known around the world. After more time, the crowd got bored and turned ugly. Their words became dangerous, bruising and tearing her young flesh. They left her in a ditch, broken and bloody.

Eventually, she found the strength to climb out. And to the artist's surprise, she was greeted with cheers and kind words from the same people who had left her to die. They called this resurrection from obscurity her "comeback tour."

· 94 ·

Fresh Catch

Jules knew his fish, from catfish to striped marlins. But he hadn't known no fish like this. Long, black, and with two mouths. Even stranger, it kicked his arm with a nubbish leg. Back in the bayou, he woulda thrown it back, but this was the Navy. Orders were orders. He pulled up huge nets of weirder fish for the next week. For testing, he was told. He thought about the mushroom cloud he had seen a couple weeks prior. People gibbered about it changing things. End the war, maybe. Well, looks like it changing more than that, Jules thought.

· 95 ·

In Our Nature

A couple's lovely afternoon on the veranda was brought to a startling halt by the sudden appearance of a foreign life-form. It was red with big eyes and about the size of a peanut (shelled).

"What the hell is that?" said Jessica.

"I don't know," said Ava. The creature inched closer and made a harsh chirp.

Jessica gasped. "Kill it!" Ava snatched a stray flip-flop. Recognizing the threat to its tiny life, the creature scurried away. Ava chased it down and relentlessly beat it with her shoe until nothing was left except a yellow pulp.

"Got it, babe," she said.

· 96 ·

Confidence

He sits at the back of the comic shop, reading his recent sci-fi story aloud to a group of unique and talented writers. He's worked for months on this story and feels sort of proud. "They hate it," he thinks. He reads a particularly humorous line. The group laughs. "That joke wasn't funny. That was a pity laugh." He dreads hearing their feedback. He finishes and receives positive comments with constructive criticism. "Are they just being nice?" That night, he lies awake in bed. "I bet that's it. They lied. They should've been honest with me. I could've handled it."

· 97 ·

The Other Woman

After a late night at work, John returned home, undressed, and got into bed with his already-asleep wife, Kelly. Then he heard something shift under the bed. He hoped it was only his mind playing tricks on him. He reached to Kelly for comfort, gently rousing her from her slumber. Kelly's back felt strangely squishy. "Yes, my dear husband?" she said, shifting between pitches with each syllable as if trying to find the correct tone. Before John could reply, a hand covered his mouth. He turned. It was Kelly, the real Kelly, kneeling beside the bed with a finger to her lips.

· 98 ·

Decisions

Overwhelmed by the assortment of desserts, Kylie asks Mary her preference.

"The chocolate pie is my favorite," says Mary. Kylie chooses the pie, and they sit at a table for two. "The appointment went well?" Mary asks. Kylie struggles to balance some pie on her fork.

"Yeah." Taking a bite, Kylie hides her mouth as she chews. A young boy catches her eye.

Mary sips her espresso. "How far along are you?"

Kylie takes another bite, "Fourteen weeks."

Savoring another sip, Mary smiles, "You're doing an amazing thing for me, you know." Kylie keeps her head low and swallows hard.

· 99 ·

Cloud Shaper

Do you know how clouds are made? They are made by the shapers. Beings older than any god. Heat from the sunkeeper gifts them water in the form of vapor. Taking the vapor, the shaper, with invisible hands, molds the saturated air like a person does clay. But the work of the cloud shapers is only temporary. Every minute their creations shift and fade. Eventually, their art will disappear, its medium recycled to create new things. So when you watch the clouds, make sure to appreciate every puffy clump or lacy ruffle. What you see may never be seen again.

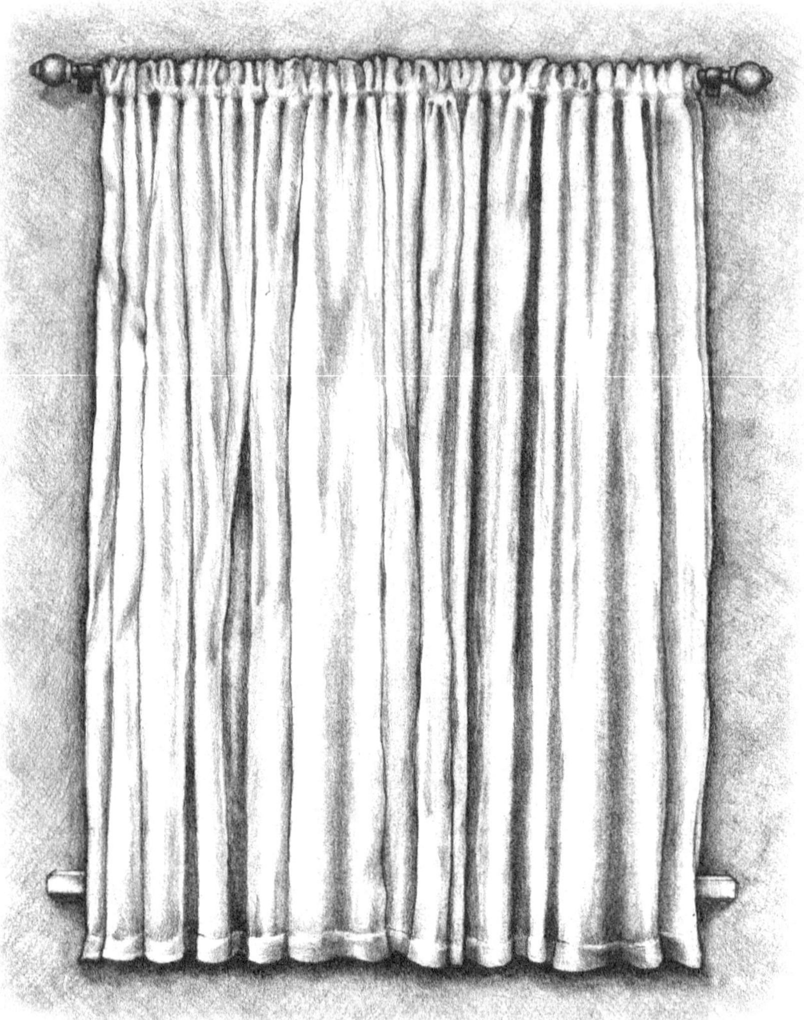

· 100 ·

The End

The window has shown me many things. Left me with both new and familiar perspectives. Some stories make me smile or keep me up at night. While other tales bring a tear, a laugh, or a memory. Not every world I hope to see again. Some linger in my mind. Maybe one day the window will allow me to return to those worlds, to see more. But for now, the light is gone and the day is ending. I put my notebook away and close the curtains. When tomorrow greets me, I will take whatever it and the window bring.

Meet the Author

James Dupree is a writer specializing in short fiction. When not writing, he can be found harvesting fresh fruit and herbs on a family farm, baking things, or staring out windows. You can find more of his work on Instagram @jamesmdupree. He lives in Chapel Hill, North Carolina with his partner and furry children.

Meet the Illustrator

Kathleen Dupree is a graphic designer/ illustrator, a fruit and herb farmer, and mother of the author (her proudest accomplishment, says she.) She lives a happy, contented life on the farm where she designs and illustrates greeting cards, picks fruit and grows herbs. You can find more of her work on Instagram @feathervillagefarm and @dupree.katie.82 and kdgraphic.redbubble.com